Jordan thought he was going to burst with rage. How dare Alex Jackson steal all his best jokes, and pretend to be him? It wasn't fair. It was disgusting. It was outrageous. It was probably against the law.

It's the best joke ever! The schoolteachers have got Alex and Jordan mixed up and think that meek maths genius Alex is cheeky troublemaker Jordan. So why not let them go on thinking that while the boys have some fun? But when Alex begins to enjoy the switch a bit too much, and starts to act as if he really is Jordan, things start to go wrong . . .

Narinder Dhami was born in Wolverhampton. She lives in Cambridge with her husband and four cats and when she is not writing enjoys reading, gardening, and travelling (especially to India and Italy). *Changing Places* is her first book for Oxford University Press.

Changing Places

Changing Places

Narinder Dhami

ILLUSTRATED BY JONATHAN ALLEN

OXFORD
UNIVERSITY PRESS

OXFORD
UNIVERSITY PRESS

Great Clarendon Street, Oxford OX2 6DP

Oxford University Press is a department of the University of Oxford.
It furthers the University's objective of excellence in research, scholarship,
and education by publishing worldwide in

Oxford New York

Auckland Bangkok Buenos Aires
Cape Town Chennai Dar es Salaam Delhi Hong Kong Istanbul
Karachi Kolkata Kuala Lumpur Madrid Melbourne Mexico City Mumbai
Nairobi São Paulo Shanghai Singapore Taipei Tokyo Toronto
with an associated company in Berlin

Oxford is a registered trade mark of Oxford University Press
in the UK and in certain other countries

British Library Cataloguing in Publication Data available

ISBN 0 19 275232 4

1 3 5 7 9 10 8 6 4 2

Designed and typeset by Mike Brain Graphic Design Limited, Oxford

Printed in Great Britain by Cox & Wyman Ltd

For Holly, Jade, and Amber

Chapter One

'Jordan! *Jordan!* Do you want to be late for school?'

Jordan didn't even bother to answer that. Mums always asked daft questions. As if he wanted to go to school at all, especially a new one.

His mum swished crossly into the room with the baby on her hip, and turned the TV off.

'Oh, *Mum*!' Jordan grumbled. Elastic-man had just been about to splatter the baddies all over the cartoon universe.

'School, Jordan. *Now*.' His mum pointed at

1

the door. 'Or do you want me to come with you?'

'No, thanks,' Jordan said quickly. It wasn't cool to arrive at a new school with your mum. That sort of thing could ruin your reputation for years to come. Reluctantly he got up from the sofa, pulling down his new sweatshirt. It was a horrible blue colour, and *Maple Bank Junior* was embroidered on it in a sick-making yellow. Jordan hoped his mum wouldn't notice that he'd already spilt Coco Pops down it.

'And, Jordan . . . '

'Yeah?' Jordan stopped at the door of the flat.

'Be good,' his mum said wearily.

'Sure,' Jordan replied, giving her and the baby a cheery wave. 'See ya.'

'49 times 58 . . . ' Alexander Jackson paused for a moment and frowned. '2,842.'

He checked the sum on the calculator and grinned triumphantly, pushing his round glasses further up his nose.

'72 times 61 . . . '

'Alex, hurry up.' That was his mother calling from downstairs. 'You don't want to be late on your first day, do you?'

'No,' Alex called back. 'Coming.' He stood up and brushed down his new uniform carefully. Black trousers and blue sweatshirt with *Maple Bank Junior* in yellow. Very smart.

The Jacksons had moved house because Alex's father had a new job. That was why Alex was starting at Maple Bank Junior. Alex wondered if he was going to be the only new boy at the school, but he didn't really care if he was. Even if he didn't make any friends, the teachers would love him. They always did.

'We're really going to miss you, Alex,' Mrs Peachey, his old headteacher, had said on his last day in July. There had even been tears in her eyes. Alex had been very flattered at the time, even if it was because Kingston Primary wouldn't have a hope of winning the local Junior Schools Maths Quiz without him.

'72 times 61,' he said thoughtfully as he went out of the bedroom. '4,392.'

This time he didn't even bother to check it on his calculator. He knew he was right.

'And how are we this morning?' Mrs Fine asked, breezing into the staffroom. 'Have you all had a good holiday?'

'No,' muttered Mr Graham, who was looking pale. This year he had 5J, the terrorists of Maple Bank Junior, organized and led by Big Emily Collins.

'I've been ill for the last two weeks,' sneezed Miss Patel, grabbing another tissue. 'The doctor says it's stress.'

'I'm looking for another job,' Mrs Benson said, sipping her coffee. 'Anything that doesn't involve children.'

'Good, glad to see you're all happy to be back.' The headteacher wasn't listening. She was homing in like a nuclear missile on Miss Kinsella, who was making herself a cup of tea. 'Oh, Kate, I've got another new boy for you.'

Miss Kinsella looked alarmed. This year she had 4K, who were very well-behaved. Mrs

Benson, who'd had them last year, said they were so well-behaved it was like teaching a class full of crash dummies. Miss Kinsella didn't mind that at all. Crash dummies sat still and didn't cheek the teacher. She was really looking forward to it. Then, at the end of last term, Mrs Fine had told her that Alexander Jackson would be joining the class in September.

'He's brilliant at maths!' Mrs Fine had said, very excited. 'He can do long multiplication in his head!'

Miss Kinsella had been impressed. *She* couldn't do long multiplication in her head, and it was touch and go whether she could actually do it on paper. She hadn't been too worried though. It sounded as if Alexander Jackson would fit into Class 4K very well indeed. But another new boy?

'Jordan King.' Mrs Fine raised her eyebrows and lowered her voice. Miss Kinsella's heart sank. 'He's been to three different schools already. His last headteacher says he's a troublemaker.'

'Oh, really?' Miss Kinsella said bravely. 'Was he expelled from his last school?'

'Not quite,' Mrs Fine replied, grim-faced. 'Although I believe he came close to it after an incident with the headteacher's false teeth.'

Miss Kinsella felt rather faint. She could see her hope of a nice, quiet year with a nice, well-behaved class disappearing fast.

'No, his family have moved house,' Mrs Fine went on. 'That's why he's coming to Maple Bank. And I don't have to tell you, Kate—' Mrs Fine eyeballed the teacher sternly '—that Jordan King's got to learn right from the start that we won't put up with bad behaviour at Maple Bank Junior.'

'Yes, of course, Mrs Fine,' Miss Kinsella agreed in the same stern tone.

'Oh, Jan.' Mrs Fine popped her head round the door of the school office. 'Could you bring up the records on those two new boys in Kate Kinsella's class. When you've got a minute.'

'Yes, Mrs Fine.' The school secretary, Mrs

Binns, pulled a face at the door as it closed. The headteacher's *when you've got a minute* always meant *right away or else*.

'As if I haven't got enough to do!' Mrs Binns grumbled, searching through the piles of paper on her large desk. The first day of term was always a nightmare. There were twelve registers to be checked and given out. All the dinner money for the week had to be collected. Big Emily Collins in 5J always pretended she was ill so she could wag off school and go home. And of all the little ones who'd come up from the Infants, at least four were bound to wet themselves before playtime.

'*There* they are!' Mrs Binns suddenly spotted the two cardboard folders, one blue and one red, which had been sent on to Maple Bank from the boys' previous schools. The blue folder had a photo of Jordan on the front and the red one had a photo of Alex. The folders were right in the middle of a huge, teetering pile of papers and files, and as the secretary impatiently pulled them out, everything crashed to the ground.

'Oh!' Mrs Binns said a rude word under her breath. She got down on her hands and knees, and began to collect everything up. As she was piling all the papers together, she noticed that the photos had come off both folders in the muddle.

Mrs Binns didn't have any time to waste. She immediately picked up the photos, grabbed her glue pen, and stuck each one back on to the folder which was nearest, one photo on the blue and one on the red.

She didn't realize that the red folder marked *Alexander Jackson* now had a photograph of Jordan King on it, and that the blue folder marked *Jordan King* had a photo of Alex Jackson.

Chapter Two

Jordan pushed himself higher on the swing. One day he wanted to swing right over the top bar like a trapeze artist, but he hadn't quite got the nerve to try it yet. Never mind. He would some day. It was great having to go past a park on the way to school, he thought, as he swung even higher. It meant that he could practise his trapeze act every day.

'Oi!' Jordan brought the swing to a halt. A black Labrador was sniffing round his school sweatshirt which lay on the grass where he'd chucked it.

'Hey! Give that back, you stupid dog!' Jordan leapt off the swing and chased after the Labrador who was running away, trailing the sweatshirt like a banner.

'I don't believe it!' Alex's mum wailed. 'I just don't believe it!' The car was parked by the kerb, and steam was pouring out of the engine as if it was a boiling kettle. 'Today of all days!'

'Don't worry, Mum,' Alex said, hoisting his school bag on to his shoulder. 'I can walk from here.'

'But I've called the AA now,' his mum groaned. 'I'll have to stay with the car till they get here.'

'It's all right, Mum,' Alex said patiently. 'I can go on my own. I know the way.'

'But it's your first day!' Mrs Jackson looked horrified. 'What will your teacher think if I don't come with you?'

'I'll explain,' Alex said quickly. 'And you can

see my teacher when you pick me up tonight.'

'Well, all right . . . ' Mrs Jackson gave in. 'You remember what I told you, don't you? Miss Kinsella, Class 4K, and the headteacher's called Mrs Fine.' She glanced at her watch. 'Alex, you'll have to hurry or you'll be late.'

Alex was alarmed. He'd never been late for school in his life, and he didn't want to start now. Quickly he walked off in the direction of Maple Bank Junior.

* * *

'Look at that picture.' Mrs Fine gave the blue folder to Miss Kinsella. 'Look at those eyes. They're too close together. You can see Jordan King's a troublemaker at a glance, can't you?'

Miss Kinsella stared down at Alex Jackson's mild-mannered face and round glasses. 'He doesn't look quite as cheeky as I thought he would,' she said cautiously.

'Well, he's not stupid,' Mrs Fine admitted as she handed Miss Kinsella a sheet of Jordan's test scores. 'Just very lazy. And a nuisance. If I was to tell you the joke he played on his last teacher . . .' She shook her head sadly. 'Let's just say it involved a very loud whoopee cushion and the school governors.'

Miss Kinsella almost laughed, then stopped herself, horrified.

'Now Alex Jackson.' Mrs Fine passed over the red folder, and they both gazed down at Jordan's cheeky grin. 'You can tell he's intelligent and hard-working just by looking at him, can't you?'

They were standing in the corridor outside Miss Kinsella's classroom, waiting for the bell to ring. Outside, the playground was full of children, big and small. The new children who'd come up from the Infants looked terrified, while some members of 5J were already fighting behind the canteen. Big Emily Collins was winning.

The bell rang, and Miss Kinsella began to greet her new class. 4K filed into school quietly, hung their coats up quietly, and went into the classroom quietly. Miss Kinsella hoped that Jordan King would be very impressed with all this good behaviour. It might even make him behave better himself.

'Aha!' Mrs Fine's face lit up. 'Here comes Alexander Jackson now.'

Miss Kinsella glanced across the playground. A tall, dark-haired boy was coming through the gate. His muddy sweatshirt was tied in a knot round his waist, and the laces of his trainers were trailing behind him.

Miss Kinsella was rather shocked. 'He looks a bit of a mess, doesn't he?'

'My dear Kate, the boy's got other things on his mind!' Mrs Fine declared. 'He's probably working out some difficult maths problem in his head.'

Jordan was feeling hard done by. He'd chased the dog so far, he'd ended up outside the school gates. So he had no real excuse for not going in, unfortunately. Still, he thought, glancing round the empty playground, at least he was late, even if it was only by a minute. Start as you meant to go on was Jordan's motto. And he'd got his sweatshirt back, although it was now covered in teethmarks.

Jordan looked up at the school. It was one of those old, gloomy, Victorian buildings, on two floors. It didn't look very friendly or welcoming at all.

'Hello, come this way.' A door opened suddenly, and a woman popped out. She was beaming all over her face. 'Welcome to Maple Bank Junior. We're so pleased to have you at our school!'

Jordan was taken aback. Maple Bank was the fourth school he'd been to, and none of his teachers had ever said they were pleased to have him before. Sad, yes. Unhappy, yes.

Depressed, yes. But never *pleased*.

'Thanks very much,' he said cautiously. Maybe this was some kind of trick the teachers here played on all new pupils. Get them off their guard, and then hit them right between the eyes with a detention or two.

'I'm Mrs Fine, the headteacher.' This strange woman was still smiling as if she'd been waiting all her life to meet him. 'And this is your teacher, Miss Kinsella.'

'I'm very pleased to meet you, Alex,' Miss Kinsella said warmly. 'Welcome to 4K.'

Jordan began to feel very nervous. What was

wrong with all these teachers? Why were they treating him like some sort of film star? Then, suddenly, he realized. Miss Kitchen Sink or whatever her name was had called him *Alex*.

'I'm not—' he began, but Mrs Fine had put an arm round his shoulders and was guiding him towards the cloakroom.

'This is where you hang your coat up, Alex,' she was saying, 'and that's your classroom over there. 4K.'

Before Jordan could explain, the outside door opened again. A small, thin boy wearing round glasses was standing there. He was bright red in the face.

'Sorry . . . I'm . . . late,' Alex wheezed with difficulty. He'd taken a wrong turning and had to run. Now he'd spoilt his 100 per cent record of never being late, he thought crossly.

'Oh, there you are,' Mrs Fine remarked rather coldly. 'Welcome to Maple Bank Junior, Jordan. I hope you're not going to make a habit of being late.'

Alex stared blankly at her. 'I'm . . . not—' he began between breaths.

'Hi, Jordan,' Jordan interrupted quickly. He was silently laughing fit to bust. This was the best joke ever. 'I'm new too. I'm Alex.'

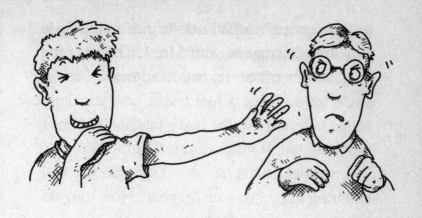

Chapter Three

'What do you think you're *doing*?' Alex spluttered. He was furious. The day had started badly, and was getting worse. Not only was he late for school, he had somehow turned into someone else.

Jordan could hardly speak for laughing.

'This is great. They think I'm you and you're me!'

'I guessed that,' Alex muttered. They were in the cloakroom, taking off their coats. Alex had tried to explain the mistake, but being so out of breath, he hadn't managed to get the words out quickly enough. Miss Kinsella had disappeared into the classroom, and Mrs Fine had gone back to her office. As the headteacher went, she'd given Alex a *look*. Alex was shocked. Never before in his life had a teacher looked at him like that. It made him feel quite ill.

'I wonder how it happened.' Jordan was still laughing as he hung up his coat. 'How long do you reckon we can fool them?'

'What?' Alex glared at Jordan. 'Don't be stupid. We're going to tell them *right now*.'

'No, we're not,' Jordan retorted. 'This is a great laugh!'

'It is not!' Alex was hardly able to speak, he was so furious. 'I'm going to tell Miss Kinsella she's made a mistake!'

Jordan didn't answer. For the first time he looked at Alex properly. Spotless uniform, brand-new school bag, clean fingernails. He even wore shoes, not trainers, and they'd been *polished*. Jordan guessed that Alex had never been in trouble with a teacher in his life.

'And what if I don't want to?' he asked in a slightly menacing tone.

Alex gulped. Jordan was a lot bigger than he was, and he looked scary. Alex had had problems with bullies at school before. He seemed to attract them like bees to honey.

'You've got to!' he said in a voice that squeaked a bit.

'I haven't *got* to do anything.' Jordan wasn't really a bully. But this was a fantastic joke, and he wasn't prepared to give it up just because Alex was a wimp.

'Yes, you have,' Alex said weakly.

'No, I haven't.' Jordan took one step towards him, and Alex scuttled out of reach, looking scared.

'But . . . but you can't be me forever!' he gabbled nervously. 'The teachers'll soon find out, even if we don't tell them.'

Jordan winked at him. 'We'll see!' he said, and went into the classroom. Alex grabbed his bag and followed him, boiling with fury. How *dare* Jordan pretend to be him? It wasn't fair. It was disgusting. It was outrageous. It was probably against the law.

'Oh, Jordan, Alex, do come in.' Miss Kinsella

was giving out pens, pencils, and new books to a silent 4K. 'I thought you might like to sit together as you're both new.' She pointed out two chairs at a table in the middle of the room.

'Thanks, Miss.' Jordan sat down in one of the empty chairs, and patted the other one. 'Come on, Jordan.'

Alex almost burst with rage. 'I'm not sitting next to HIM!' he roared.

'Oh!' The whole of 4K gasped with amazement, and Miss Kinsella turned pink. She had to be tough with Jordan King right away, or Mrs Fine would not be pleased.

'Jordan!' she said sharply. 'Do as you're told and sit down next to Alex.'

Alex almost fainted when he realized what he'd done. He'd never been rude to a teacher. Never in his life.

'Sorry, Miss,' he muttered, turning bright red. But Miss Kinsella had stalked angrily over to the cupboard, and didn't hear him.

'You'd better watch out, Jordan,' Jordan said cheerfully as Alex slumped into the chair next to him. 'You'll get into trouble if you cheek the teacher!'

'Oh, shut up!' Alex muttered under his breath. He would just have to find a way of telling Miss Kinsella the truth without Jordan finding out.

Meanwhile, Jordan was getting to know the other two children at the table, a red-headed boy with teeth like Bugs Bunny and a girl who was nervously chewing a strand of her long fair hair.

'Hi, I'm Alex,' Jordan said breezily, and Alex shot him a dirty look. 'This is Jordan.'

'I am not—' Alex began, then shut up

quickly as Jordan shot *him* a look. 'Hello,' he said feebly.

The boy and girl seemed too frightened to say anything. They were both staring at Alex as if he'd hypnotized them.

'You'd better watch out, mate,' Jordan said with a wink. 'You're scaring 4K!'

Alex had to bite his lip to stop himself saying something rude. He waited impatiently for a while until everyone was moving around, putting their new books away. Jordan had been watching him while they were writing their names on their new books and folders, so Alex had had to write *Jordan King* on all of them. He'd even had to put his books away in the drawer labelled *Jordan King*. Alex was so mad, he couldn't stand it a minute longer. He slid out of his seat, and crept over to Miss Kinsella's table.

'Miss, can I talk to you?' Alex muttered out of the side of his mouth. He kept a sharp eye on Jordan, who was putting his books away in the drawer labelled *Alex Jackson*.

'What?' Miss Kinsella frowned.

'I said, can I talk to you?' Alex muttered.

He spoke without moving his lips, like a ventriloquist.

'Jordan, is this some kind of joke?' Miss Kinsella said crossly. 'I can't hear a word you're saying.'

'Look inside my sweatshirt, Miss,' Alex mumbled. He was trying to twist the neck of the sweatshirt round so that Miss Kinsella

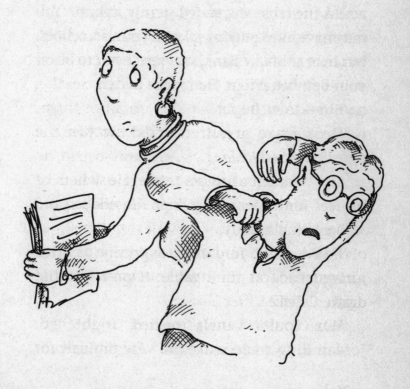

could see the nametag his mum had sewn inside. But it was so tight he almost choked himself.

Miss Kinsella threw up her eyes. 'Go and sit down, Jordan,' she snapped.

'I'm not Jordan,' Alex said desperately through his teeth. But it sounded like 'Um no Judan.'

'Now look here, Jordan.' Miss Kinsella leaned across the table and stared sternly at him. 'You may have liked playing jokes at your last school, but here at Maple Bank, we expect you to be on your best behaviour. Do I make myself clear?'

'But—' Alex began.

'Do I make myself clear?' Miss Kinsella repeated crossly.

Alex was about to protest again when he noticed Jordan watching them. He nodded and walked off gloomily.

'I saw you,' Jordan said grimly as Alex arrived back at their table. 'Don't try that again. Or else.'

Alex couldn't help feeling frightened. Jordan King could make life very difficult for him if he wanted to. Alex had had enough experience of bullies at his previous school to know that.

'She didn't believe me anyway,' he muttered.

Jordan's face split into a big grin. 'This is so cool!'

Alex stared at him. He just couldn't understand it. What was cool about pretending to be someone else and fooling the teachers? Why was it such a great laugh?

'What jokes did you play at your last school?' he asked, suddenly remembering what Miss Kinsella had said.

Jordan shrugged. 'Loads,' he replied casually.

'Like what?' Alex wanted to know. If the teachers thought he was Jordan King, he needed to have some idea of what he was up against.

'I put a whoopee cushion on my teacher's chair when the school governors visited our classroom.' Jordan chuckled at the memory. 'That was pretty funny. Oh, and there was all that stuff with Mr Barker's false teeth. I nearly got expelled for that.'

'It's time for assembly,' Miss Kinsella said.

'Put your books away and line up by the door quietly, please. No talking.'

'What happened with Mr Barker's false teeth?' Alex asked suddenly. Then he blushed. Everyone else was lining up quietly by the door, and he was the only person in the whole classroom who was talking.

'I said *quietly*, Jordan,' Miss Kinsella reminded him in a cold voice.

Alex turned even redder. He'd never hit anyone in his whole life, but he felt like punching Jordan King on the nose as the other boy grinned jauntily at him. How could everything be going wrong like this?

'Playtime will be straight after assembly,' Miss Kinsella informed them, opening the classroom door. 'And after playtime we'll be doing maths, so I want you all to get your books and maths equipment out as soon as you come in.'

Alex's heart lifted immediately. As he lined up behind Jordan, he grinned to himself. Of course. Why hadn't he thought of it before? It was so obvious. He was Alex Jackson, and he was fantastic at maths. Jordan King couldn't be half as fantastic at maths as he was. So when Miss Kinsella gave him some really difficult sums to do, Jordan wouldn't have a clue. Then everyone would find out at last who the *real* Alex Jackson was.

Alex couldn't wait to see Jordan King try and get out of this one.

Chapter Four

Alex stomped out into the playground. He was *furious*. All he'd done was *accidentally* set off his watch alarm, just before assembly started. Anyone would think he'd *murdered* somebody.

Everyone in 4K had jumped a mile in the air, and stared at him in horror, except for Jordan King, of course. He'd just sniggered. Miss Kinsella had risen from her chair at the side of the hall, and fixed Alex with a steely glare.

'Jordan King!' she'd hissed. 'Come and sit next to me, where I can keep an eye on you.'

'But, Miss—' Alex protested.

'*Now!*' Miss Kinsella cut in fiercely, just as Mrs Fine swept into the hall.

So Alex had to climb to his feet and make his way to the end of the row, while everyone watched disapprovingly. Then he'd had to sit right next to Miss Kinsella for the whole assembly, as if he was some *baby* who didn't know how to behave himself.

Alex was so angry, he didn't know what to do with himself. He kicked at a Coca-Cola can lying on the ground, then he jumped furiously up and down on it until he'd crushed it flat. A group of Year 3 children stopped to stare at him.

'What're *you* staring at?' Alex snapped.

The Year 3 kids looked alarmed. This new boy was *strange*. Quickly they ran off to the other side of the playground.

'Hello, *Jordan*.' Grinning from ear to ear, the real Jordan King strolled over to Alex. 'How're you doing?'

'Oh, just great,' Alex spluttered. 'Miss

Kinsella thinks I'm a troublemaker. I'm getting picked on all the time. Everyone hates me. I'm doing just fine.'

Jordan gave him a thumbs-up sign. 'Didn't I tell you it was a great joke?'

'Do I look like I'm laughing?' Alex roared.

'You know, that's your problem,' Jordan said airily, slapping Alex on the back. 'You're too serious. You need to have a laugh.'

Alex slumped onto the grass, and put his head in his hands.

'I'll have to leave this school,' he muttered. 'I can't stay here.'

'What? Don't be so stupid.' Puzzled, Jordan stared at Alex. He honestly couldn't see what the other boy was getting so worked up about. 'Everyone'll think we're so cool when they find out the truth. Well, not the teachers, but everyone else. You'll make loads of friends.'

Alex raised his head and looked uncertainly at Jordan. He'd never had 'loads of friends'. Most children didn't want to be friends with him because he was so good at maths. Alex had discovered, painfully, that they didn't like people who were different. He'd been mates with Kevin Thomas at Kingston Primary, but that had mostly been because Kevin had needed Alex to help him with his maths. Or rather, he'd got Alex to *do* his maths for him. And he hadn't been very friendly towards Alex when he'd been hanging out with his other mates. In fact, Alex had a definite suspicion that it was Kevin Thomas who'd started the *Freaky Four-Eyes* nickname, which had dogged Alex until the day he left.

'I've been to millions of schools before this one,' Jordan went on confidently. 'Well, three anyway. So I know all about making friends.'

'Three schools?' Alex repeated. 'Why? Were you expelled?'

'No, I wasn't,' Jordan said indignantly. 'My mum keeps moving house. She calls it making a fresh start.' He shrugged. 'Maybe it'll work this time. This is the only school where the teachers haven't started on me the minute I walked through the door.'

'That's because they think you're me,' Alex said through gritted teeth. 'Anyway, don't you know that teachers talk to each other? And they keep records about us. They send them on to your next school when you leave.'

Jordan's mouth dropped open. 'They don't!'

'Of *course* they do,' Alex said impatiently. 'The teachers knew all about you before you even got here this morning.'

'Teachers are so sneaky,' Jordan grumbled. 'It's just not fair.'

'Well, you should have thought of that before you started messing around,' Alex snapped. He pulled himself to his feet as the bell rang. 'And anyway, it's me who's getting picked on now, because they think I'm you.'

But not for long, Alex added silently, as he turned and walked off. They had a maths lesson coming up. There was only one *real* Alex Jackson, maths genius, and everyone was about to find out exactly who that was. Jordan King's time was almost up.

Jordan stared down at the paper in front of him. This was maths? It was so complicated, it was sending him cross-eyed. And what did *a* and *b* and *x* and *y* have to do with sums? They were letters, not numbers. Was Miss Kinsella playing a joke on him?

'I hope you don't find these *too* easy, Alex,' she'd said, handing him the work. 'Let's see how you get on.'

Jordan rubbed his eyes, and looked up. Alex was sitting watching him, arms folded. He had a smug smile on his face.

'You can't do them, can you?' he said gleefully.

Jordan glanced sideways at Jack and Zoe, who were sitting there, goggle-eyed, taking in everything that was going on. ''Course I can,' he said bravely.

'No, you can't.' Alex turned to Jack and Zoe. 'He can't do them because he's not me,' he explained. '*I'm* really Alex Jackson, and *he's* Jordan King. That's why he can't do the sums.'

Jack and Zoe stared at Alex as if he was mad. Jordan shook his head sadly.

'Take no notice of Jordan,' he told them. 'He's just jealous because I'm a maths genius.'

Jack and Zoe looked silently impressed.

'Go on then.' Alex pointed at the first sum. 'Let's see you do *that*.'

Jordan squirmed uncomfortably in his chair. If Jack and Zoe weren't there, he could have swapped books with Alex, and they could have done each other's maths. Miss Kinsella had given Alex much easier sums, sums that Jordan knew he could do. Now he'd have to come up with another plan. He just didn't know what it was going to be yet.

'Jack and Zoe, you have some measuring work

to do,' Miss Kinsella called from the other side of the room. 'Come over here, and I'll help you.'

'Yes!' Jordan said triumphantly under his breath. He waited until Jack and Zoe had gone, then he grabbed Alex's maths book and put his own in its place.

Alex raised his eyebrows. 'What are you doing?'

'You do my sums, and I'll do yours,' Jordan said cheekily. 'Simple.'

'Oh no.' Alex folded his arms. 'No way.'

Jordan shrugged. 'Well, if they're too hard for you, just say so.'

'What do you mean?' Alex hissed angrily. 'Too hard for me? I could do those sums standing on my head, with one hand tied behind my back!'

'Yeah. Right.' Jordan reached for the maths book again. 'Don't worry about it, Alex. These sums are *really* hard, you know.'

'Get off.' Alex smacked Jordan's hand away. 'I can do these sums in five minutes flat,' he snapped, picking up his pencil. 'Just watch me.'

'Sure.' Jordan grinned to himself. He took a

rolled-up comic out of his back pocket, spread it out on his knees under the table and began to read. He had plenty of time to do Alex's sums. He could have a bit of a rest first.

Alex frowned. Hang on a minute, he thought. This shouldn't be happening. Things weren't going his way at all. He was supposed to be showing everyone that Jordan was a fake and a fraud, not doing his maths for him. Well, maybe there was still a way . . .

Alex looked at the first sum, and did some quick working-out in his head. The answer was 14. Easy. Glancing sideways at Jordan, he wrote '17' in the answer box.

Alex didn't like writing down the wrong answers. It made him feel very uncomfortable. But when Miss Kinsella marked the maths, she'd realize that something was rather odd, and then the truth would come out. Luckily, Jordan was too stupid to realize that he was filling in the wrong answers.

Jordan turned a page of his comic. 'Not filling in the wrong answers, are you?' he remarked.

Alex blushed. He couldn't help it. 'No,' he squeaked.

'Doesn't matter if you are.' Jordan shrugged and yawned. 'I'll just say that the sums were too hard for me.' He grinned. 'Then everyone will think that maybe Alex Jackson isn't such a maths genius after all.'

Jordan King was really starting to get on his nerves, Alex thought savagely. He had an answer for *everything*. Gloomily he rubbed out '17' and filled in '14' instead.

Twenty minutes later, Alex had done four pages of Jordan's difficult maths. Jordan had read his comic from cover to cover, and was just thinking about doing some of Alex's easier sums when he spied Miss Kinsella making her way across the room towards them. Quickly he grabbed his book, and tossed the other one back to Alex.

'Excellent,' Miss Kinsella beamed, as she ticked sum after sum in Jordan's maths book. 'Well done, Alex.'

'Thank you, Miss,' said Jordan and Alex together.

Miss Kinsella stopped marking, and glared at Alex. 'Are you trying to be funny, Jordan?' she asked frostily. Then her eye fell on Alex's maths book. 'Have you done *any* sums this morning?' she enquired in an even icier tone.

'Yes, Miss, I have,' Alex said indignantly.

'Well, they seem to have vanished off the face of the earth.' Miss Kinsella picked up Alex's

maths book and leafed through it. 'Go and sit at the table next to my desk. Maybe then you'll get some work done.'

Feeling very hard done by, Alex swept his maths book and pencil case into his arms, and stomped off across the classroom. The single table next to Miss Kinsella's desk was obviously the 'naughty' table, Alex thought bitterly. Reserved for children who talked too much and didn't do any work. How embarrassing that he, Alex Jackson, maths whizz-kid, should be sent to the 'naughty' table.

But maybe it wasn't all bad. Alex grinned to himself. He wouldn't be doing any more of Jordan's maths for him. And Miss Kinsella would soon get suspicious when all of a sudden, 'Alex' couldn't get his maths right.

'Alex, you've worked so hard, you can read until lunchtime,' Miss Kinsella said to Jordan. 'Put your maths book away, and go and choose a book from the class library.'

Jordan bounced up from his seat, looking relieved. He winked at Alex, and then strolled over to the bookshelves.

Alex sat bolt upright, speechless with fury. Jordan King had got away with it *again*. And now Alex was *really* angry. If no one could be bothered to listen to him, if no one could be bothered to hear the truth, then *he* wasn't going to bother either. He wasn't even going to try to tell the teachers what was going on.

Alex Jackson had finally had it with Maple Bank Junior School.

Chapter Five

Alex looked at the last sum on the page. 12 x 12. Muttering to himself, Alex wrote in the answer. 1,212.

Oh, yes, of course he knew it was *wrong*. All the sums he'd filled in were wrong. 12 x 8= 128. 11 x 7 = 117. 15 x 10 = 1,510. Alex just didn't care any more. Across the room, Jordan was stretched out on a beanbag in the sun, reading a book about dinosaurs, while Alex was sitting at the 'naughty' table, doing stupid sums. Alex ground his teeth together. It just wasn't *fair*.

He turned over the page. More easy sums.

If you had 72 sweets, and you shared them between yourself and five of your friends, how many sweets would each person have?

Alex sucked the end of his pencil, and wrote *If I had 72 sweets, I wouldn't share them. I'd eat them all myself.*

He'd started to enjoy himself now. What was the next question?

Mr Smith is going to visit his friend, Mr Brown. Mr Smith walks 5.5 kilometres an hour. Mr Brown lives 11 kilometres away. How long will it take Mr Smith to walk to Mr Brown's house?

Alex knew the answer immediately.

Mr Smith should buy a car, he wrote. *He'd get there a lot quicker.*

Alex chuckled to himself. He wasn't just good at maths, his jokes weren't bad either. Miss Kinsella would go mad, but Alex didn't care. What did it matter? No one knew who he really was, anyway. As far as they were concerned, he was Jordan King, and Jordan King was bad news. Alex was just playing his part properly.

Alex threw down his pencil, and tipped his chair right back, until it was balancing on only two of the legs. Alex had never done that in his life before. His old teacher at Kingston Primary, Mrs Tate, had told gruesome tales of children falling backwards and splitting their heads open. But Alex wasn't bothered. Anyway, balancing a chair on two legs was somehow the sort of thing that Jordan King *would* do.

Alex wondered how long Jordan could keep all this going. Surely someone would realize sooner or later? Or maybe they wouldn't. Maybe he and Jordan would be each other until they grew up. Alex thought about that. Perhaps it wasn't such a bad thing. Being Alex Jackson wasn't all that great, sometimes . . .

Bzzzzzzzzzz.

Alex jerked his head up sharply. A wasp had just flown in through the open window next to Miss Kinsella's desk.

Alex hated wasps. Kevin Thomas and his gang at Kingston Primary had thought it was great fun to make buzzing noises behind Alex's back, and see him jump a mile. But this was a real wasp. It had chosen Alex as its first victim, and was buzzing straight towards him.

'Yeeargh!' Alex roared, as the wasp swooped past his nose. He lost his balance, and the chair tipped right over.

Bloodthirsty tales of split heads flashed through Alex's mind again as he fell backwards. But luckily, the back of the chair hit Miss Kinsella's desk, and stopped. Unluckily, the chair knocked against a huge pile of maths books, unmarked stories, and folders. The whole, enormous heap was pushed off the desk.

They fell around Alex with an almighty crash.

Everyone in the room nearly leapt out of their skins. Miss Kinsella gasped, and dropped the pile of books she was holding. Most of them landed on her foot.

Jack swung round and poked Zoe in the stomach with the metre stick. Zoe burst into tears.

Jordan fell off the beanbag and hit his head on the floor, and the wasp, looking quite satisfied with what it had achieved, buzzed its way out of the window.

4K held their breath as Miss Kinsella advanced across the classroom towards Alex. Miss Kinsella was limping a bit, but she still looked scary.

'There was a wasp, Miss,' Alex began.

Miss Kinsella looked slowly and deliberately round the classroom. 'There is no wasp in this room, Jordan,' she declared.

'Not now there isn't,' Alex explained. 'It flew out of the window.'

Jordan rubbed his head, and grinned to himself. Alex had no idea how to deal with angry teachers. He might be a maths genius, but he wasn't the brightest star in the sky.

'You-will-go-and-stand-outside-in-the-corridor,' Miss Kinsella said to Alex through clenched teeth. 'And after you've had lunch, you will go straight to the detention room and write lines. Do I make myself clear?'

Everyone in 4K, including Jordan, fixed their eyes on Alex, as he stood up. Alex felt quite important. Was this what it felt like to be a film star or a pop star? Having everyone watching your every move? Alex hooked his thumbs into his belt loops, and strolled over to the door. Taking his time, he reached for the door handle, opened it, and went outside as slowly as he could.

Today was a day of firsts, Alex thought, as he leaned against the corridor wall. The first time he'd been rude to a teacher. The first time he'd been told off in class, *and* in assembly. The first time he'd got a detention. The first time he'd been sent out of class. At this rate, he'd be expelled by the end of the day. And he didn't even *care*.

Footsteps were coming along the corridor towards him. Alex turned round, and blinked. This girl was big.

Big Emily Collins was on her way back to 5J's classroom after a trip to the loo. So far she'd managed to take seventeen minutes. Her record was twenty-nine minutes and thirteen seconds, but that had been set when 5J had a supply teacher last year. Big Emily was hoping to beat her record, but she had to be careful. Today was 5J's first day with Mr Graham, and he was handing out detentions like sweets. But Big Emily would soon lick him into shape. She had lots of ideas for jokes to play on her new teacher. Big Emily liked playing jokes. She liked that almost better than bullying people.

Big Emily spotted Alex ahead of her. She saw a small, thin, weedy little boy with round glasses perched on the end of his nose. Big Emily grinned. She could have some fun with this one.

'Who's been a naughty boy then?' Big Emily said, putting her hands on her hips.

'Are you talking to me?' Alex shot back.

'No, the wall,' Big Emily said sarcastically. 'Why did you get sent out of class?'

Alex ignored her.

'I'm talking to you,' Big Emily snapped, slowly turning red in the face.

'Oh.' Alex raised his eyebrows. 'I thought you said you were talking to the wall.'

Big Emily frowned. This boy was being cheeky. People didn't cheek Big Emily and get away with it. Oh no.

Big Emily drew herself up to her full height. 'Do you know who I am?' she asked in a terrifying voice.

Alex looked bored. 'Should I?'

'I'm Big Emily Collins,' Emily snarled.

Alex shrugged. 'So?'

'Emily Collins!' Mr Graham was standing in the doorway of 5J's classroom, further down the corridor. 'Are you intending to come back to class or not?'

'I suppose so,' Big Emily replied sulkily, staying where she was.

'Today, or some time next week?' Mr Graham

enquired acidly, folding his arms. Big Emily
sighed.

'Later,' she said menacingly to Alex under
her breath.

Alex shrugged. 'Whatever.' He didn't look
frightened. He didn't even look interested.

Big Emily swelled with fury. If Mr Graham
hadn't been watching her, she'd have grabbed
that annoying pip-squeak and stuffed his head
down the loo. The cheek of him. Big Emily had
been planning to feel ill and wag off school for
the afternoon, but not any more. She was
going to stick around and teach this mouthy
little creep a lesson.

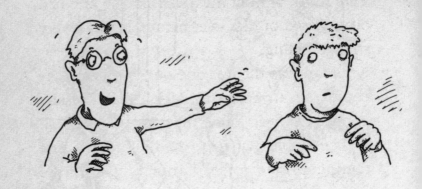

Chapter Six

The dinner bell rang. Alex yawned and cheered up a bit. It was boring standing out in the corridor, and he was starving.

Classroom doors opened, and children began to pour out. They all stared at Alex, and muttered to each other. Alex knew what they were saying. He must be *bad* to get sent out of class on his very first day at a new school.

4K filed quietly out of the classroom. They all stared at Alex too, but Alex was delighted to see that when he stared back, every one of them dropped their eyes or looked away. They were *scared* of him, Alex realized. No one had been scared of him ever before. It was a very strange feeling.

Jordan was the last one out, but before he could say anything to Alex, Miss Kinsella popped her head round the door.

'Remember what I said, Jordan,' she reminded Alex coldly. 'After lunch you go straight up to the detention room. Jack or Zoe will show you where it is.'

'Yeah, yeah,' Alex said rudely.

Miss Kinsella looked annoyed, but she was dying to head upstairs to the staffroom for a cup of coffee, so she let it go.

'What're you up to?' Jordan asked curiously, as he followed Alex down the corridor.

'I don't know what you're talking about,' Alex said coolly. He strolled out into the playground, with Jordan scurrying along behind him.

'You're really getting on Miss Kinsella's nerves,' Jordan pointed out. 'She's never going to leave you alone now.'

'So?' Alex shrugged. Funnily enough, he

wasn't even scared of Jordan any more, he thought. 'That's what you do, isn't it? Annoy the teachers? And I'm you, now, remember?'

Jordan stared wide-eyed at Alex's back, as the other boy strode off. What was the matter with him? He'd gone mad.

'Look, it's only a joke.' Jordan rushed after Alex, and grabbed him by the shoulder. 'You're not really me, you know.'

'But maybe I'm having more fun being you than being boring old Alex Jackson,' Alex said.

Jordan felt a rush of anger. 'You're *not* me!' he snapped. He was beginning to feel as if he was losing control of the situation. 'This is just a joke.'

'And I'm having a great laugh,' Alex replied with an evil smile. 'Aren't you?'

Jordan gritted his teeth. He wasn't sure at the moment.

There was a crowd of 4K children standing together near the canteen. Jack and Zoe were in the middle of it. They were telling the others what it was like to sit on the same table as Jordan King, the naughty new boy.

'So you *can* talk.' Alex pushed his way into the middle of the crowd. 'I was beginning to think you were all a load of dummies.' He reached over and took a crisp from Jack's bag of cheese-and-onion.

'Here, have them all,' Jack said, staring at Alex with round, respectful eyes.

'Thanks.' Alex took the bag, and finished off the crisps. The children watched him in silence. Meanwhile, Jordan hovered around on the edge of the crowd. He wasn't quite sure why, but he felt he ought to keep an eye on Alex.

'So, when do we get our lunch then?' Alex asked, handing the empty bag back to Jack.

'It's Year 3 first today,' Zoe told him timidly.

Alex snorted in disgust. 'I bet I could walk in there and pretend to be a Year 3 kid and get my dinner right now,' he said confidently. 'Shall I?'

'You wouldn't dare,' Jordan scoffed, as the listening children gasped in admiration.

'Why not?' Alex eyeballed Jordan through the crowd. 'It'd be a great laugh. You're just a wimp.'

'Hey, hang on a minute,' Jordan began crossly, but no one was listening to him. Most of 4K were now crowding round Alex, hanging on his every word.

'I played loads of jokes at my last school,' Alex was boasting. 'I put a whoopee cushion on my teacher's chair when the school governors visited our classroom. Now *that* was funny.'

'What!' Jordan yelled. 'I told *you* that!'

Everyone ignored him.

'What else did you do?' Jack asked breathlessly.

Alex thought quickly. 'I took my headmaster's false teeth, and put them in the secretary's cup of coffee,' he said. 'Did she scream when she got to the bottom!'

Everyone laughed. Meanwhile, Jordan was dancing up and down furiously, trying to get a word in edgeways.

'That wasn't what I did at all!' he shouted. 'What I did was—'

The crowd of children turned round and glared at him. 'Ssh!'

Jordan thought he was going to burst with rage. How *dare* Alex Jackson steal all his best jokes, and pretend to be him? It wasn't fair. It was disgusting. It was outrageous. It was probably against the law.

'I put a stinkbomb in my teacher's car,' Alex went on. He was getting so fired up now, he could almost *believe* that he'd done all these things. 'I painted all the tables in our classroom green. I stole the school hamster and left a ransom note in its cage. I—'

'Kids' stuff,' said a loud voice behind them.

4K drew in their breath in horror. Big Emily Collins was standing on the edge of the crowd, next to Jordan. Her arms were folded, and she looked ready to kill somebody. Her gang of mates stood around, sniggering.

Who's *this*? Jordan thought. He looked Big Emily up and down. Very scary. Alex had better watch himself here.

'What did you say?' Alex demanded.

'I said, kids' stuff.' Big Emily pushed her way forward, treading heavily on Jordan's foot in the process.

'Aargh!' Jordan yelled. He hopped frantically around, clutching his injured toe. But no one took any notice of him at all. Their eyes were fixed on Big Emily and Alex.

'You wouldn't know a good joke if it bit you on the bottom,' Big Emily said rudely to Alex. 'My jokes are the best in this school.' Big Emily swelled with pride. 'Last year I sneaked into the canteen, and put one hundred plastic flies in the mashed potato. Mrs Fine said it was the most disgusting thing she'd ever seen or heard of.'

'Is that the best you can do?' Alex asked coolly.

Big Emily's large hands bunched into fists. 'You're dead!' she roared.

'Ohhhhhh!' 4K huddled together, looking terrified, as Big Emily loomed furiously over Alex. Jordan groaned. Did Alex have a death wish?

One of Big Emily's mates nudged her. 'Go on, Em,' she said, 'tell him about the flagpole.'

Big Emily smiled wolfishly. 'Last year I went round the back of the school, climbed right up on to the flat roof extension, and ran Miss Patel's coat up the school flagpole,' she said proudly.

'Easy.' Alex folded his arms. 'Anyone could do *that*.'

'*You* couldn't!' Big Emily snarled.

'Oh, yes, I could,' Alex said calmly. 'You give me your PE shorts, and I'll climb up there and run *those* up the flagpole instead.'

Chapter Seven

There was a moment of shocked silence.

'You can't!' Big Emily spluttered. 'We're not allowed round the back of the school any more. Mrs Fine said it was out of bounds after that.'

'Mrs Fine said anyone who goes round there without permission gets a month's detentions,' Jack added timidly.

Alex grinned. 'Like that's really going to stop me.' He held out his hand to Big Emily. 'PE shorts?'

Big Emily looked uncertainly at him. She

wasn't quite sure what to make of this boy. He *looked* quite small and weedy, but he seemed totally fearless.

'Forget it,' she scoffed. 'You'd never make it on to the flat roof anyway. You're too titchy.'

'Just watch me,' Alex shot back. 'Now are you going to get those PE shorts, or are you going to chicken out?'

Big Emily looked round. Everyone was watching, waiting to see what she would do. If she didn't give in, it would look as if she was *scared* of this jumped-up little twit.

'All right,' Big Emily snapped, and marched off.

Jordan groaned to himself. He'd never expected the joke to get out of hand like this. It had only been a laugh. Now Alex was heading for major trouble, and taking Jordan with him too. What if Alex hurt himself while he was trying to pull this stupid stunt? Jordan felt cold all over. Everyone would blame him. He'd be suspended. Expelled, maybe. His mum would be really mad, and they'd have to make yet another fresh start. He had to do something.

'Alex, I have to talk to you.' Jordan muscled his way through the crowd, and grabbed Alex's arm.

'Yes?' Alex blinked at him from behind his thick lenses.

'*What* are you *doing*?' Jordan snapped. 'Are you crazy? You're going to be in so much trouble—and so am I!'

'So?' Alex yawned.

Jordan grabbed Alex by the shoulders and shook him. 'Stop it!' he shouted. 'You're not me! I'm not you! This joke is over RIGHT NOW.'

Alex just laughed. Furious, Jordan spun round and spoke to the watching crowd.

'*I'm* Jordan King,' he shouted, 'and *he's* Alex Jackson. He's the maths genius, not me.'

Everyone looked blankly at him. At that moment, Big Emily came back, carrying a pair of bright pink baggy shorts.

'Let's get on with it then,' she snapped, elbowing Jordan out of the way. Jordan went flying, and ended up sprawled on the ground, with all the breath knocked out of him.

'Wait!' Jordan panted, as Alex, Emily, her friends, and most of 4K disappeared around the back of the school. 'Didn't you hear what I said?'

Painfully Jordan pulled himself to his feet, and ran round the side of the building. The dinner ladies were standing in a group, chatting, but they'd soon notice that the playground was emptier than usual. There wasn't much time.

Alex and Emily were standing next to the fire escape. The others were hovering near the corner, so that they could make a quick getaway if the dinner ladies arrived.

'Give me your shorts,' Alex said, holding out his hand. Scowling, Big Emily slapped them on to his palm. Alex shook them out and studied them.

'If I fall, I'll be able to use them as a parachute,' he remarked. 'They're big enough.'

'You cheeky little—' Big Emily began furiously. Meanwhile 4K tittered. So did Emily's mates, who then pretended they were really coughing instead.

Alex glanced up at the fire escape, plotting his route. The fire escape was quite close to the big, flat-roofed extension which had been built on to the back of the school to house the cloakrooms and toilets. It would just about be possible to get on to the roof of the extension from the stairs, Alex thought. The flagpole was attached to the main roof, but the bottom of it was close to the extension. He would just be able to reach it.

'Alex!' Jordan skidded to a halt in front of Emily and Alex. 'You're not really going to do this, are you?'

'Alex?' Big Emily looked suspicious. 'I thought your name was Jordan.'

Alex nodded. 'It is,' he said.

'No, it's not.' Jordan turned desperately to Big Emily. '*I'm* Jordan. *He's* Alex.'

Big Emily's face darkened. 'Are you trying to be funny?' she snapped.

'Look at him.' Jordan pointed at Alex. 'He can't climb up there. He's a wimp and a weed.'

'Thanks very much,' Alex said.

Big Emily smirked. All the better. She was dying to see Jordan or Alex or whatever his name was make a total idiot of himself. That'd teach him a lesson.

'I'm not going to let you do it!' Jordan said, clutching Alex's arm.

'Shut up and let him go, or I'll sit on you,' Big Emily threatened. She took one step forward, and Jordan let go of Alex's arm quickly. He wasn't going to argue with Big Emily.

Alex smiled to himself. He turned, gave the crowd a cheeky wave and ran lightly up the fire escape. That was the easy bit.

When he was almost at the top of the steps,

Alex stopped and peered over the handrail. The gap between the fire escape and the flat roof looked bigger from up here than it did on the ground. But Alex wasn't going to let that stop him. He ducked under the rail, and squinted at the gap. Could he jump across to the roof? He wasn't sure.

'He'll never make it,' Big Emily scoffed triumphantly, as Alex climbed under the handrail.

Jordan clapped his hand over his eyes. He couldn't bear to watch.

There was a cheer. Cautiously Jordan opened his eyes. Alex was standing on the flat roof, looking down at everyone.

Alex had never felt so strong and confident in his life before. It was great being someone else, being Jordan King. This was the most exciting thing he'd *ever* done, he told himself gleefully, as he ran across the flat roof to the flagpole.

Mr Graham put down his cup of coffee. That was funny, he thought. He could have sworn he'd seen a *boy* run across the flat roof, which was just outside the staffroom window. No, it couldn't be. Mr Graham sighed, and shook his head. He was seeing things now. 5J were obviously getting to him already. And it was only the first day of term.

Alex was unwinding the ropes which were wrapped around the flagpole. There was no flag flying at the moment, and it took Alex a little while to sort out which rope was which. When, finally, he found the right one, he slid it through one leg of Emily's PE shorts, and pulled. The shorts began to rise upwards. Alex grinned delightedly, and kept on pulling. A few moments later, Big Emily Collins's baggy pink shorts were fluttering in the breeze, high above the school.

There was another cheer from down below. Alex leaned over the edge of the flat roof, and gave everyone a thumbs-up sign. Big Emily was purple with rage, but Alex didn't care about her. He wasn't afraid of Big Emily. He wasn't afraid of anyone. This was the best moment of his whole life.

Hold on a moment. Why had everything suddenly gone all blurry?

Alex gasped. He clutched at the edge of the roof, and closed his eyes. His head was spinning. He'd begun to sweat. His heart was pounding.

Suddenly, Alex remembered. He'd been so busy being Jordan King, that he'd forgotten something very important about himself. About Alex Jackson.

Alex Jackson was scared of heights.

Chapter Eight

Alex clutched the edge of the flat roof as if he was never going to let go. He felt sick. Every time he opened his eyes, the faces below swam and blurred, as if he was under water. He couldn't move. His legs felt like lead.

'What's the matter with him?' Jordan asked anxiously.

'He's wimped out!' Big Emily announced, grinning all over her face. 'I knew he would!'

'Shut up.' Jordan turned on her fiercely.

'You'll be sorry you said that,' Big Emily growled, lunging forward.

Jordan side-stepped her, and ran towards the fire escape. If he could just get Alex down in one piece, they could stop this stupid joke once and for all. And he'd never play another joke as long as he lived. 'Hang on, Alex,' Jordan called. 'I'm coming.'

'I'm not going anywhere,' Alex said weakly, eyes still closed.

Jordan clattered up the steps, and crouched down to look under the handrail. 'Alex, come over here,' he called softly. Alex was still across the other side of the flat roof, near the flagpole. 'I'll help you down.'

'I can't,' Alex whimpered.

'Yes, you can,' Jordan said. He held out his hand. 'Come on.'

Shivering, Alex let go of the edge of the roof. He couldn't walk because his legs were shaking so much. So he had to crawl on his hands and knees towards Jordan.

'Ohh!' Alex groaned, as he stared down at the gap between the fire escape and the roof.

'Don't look down!' Jordan told him urgently. 'Now jump across to me.'

Alex closed his eyes.

'No, with your eyes open!' Jordan gasped. He was shaking himself, with nerves.

Alex took a deep breath, and launched himself at the fire escape. He managed to grab the handrail, but his feet missed the step, and, for a second, he was dangling in thin air. There was a gasp of horror from the children below.

'I've got you!' Jordan grabbed Alex's waist, and hauled the other boy under the handrail. Alex collapsed on the step, and buried his face in his hands.

'Come on, we've got to get out of here.' Jordan was already hurrying down the steps again. 'Before the teachers catch us.'

Alex hauled himself dizzily to his feet. What had he been thinking of? he wondered, as he clutched the handrail. He wasn't the kind of boy who did things like that. And had he really cheeked Big Emily Collins, who was standing there grinning smugly at him, without a care in the world? Alex shuddered. He must've been mad.

Jordan reached the bottom of the fire escape first. Big Emily Collins was waiting for him.

'I knew he'd wimp out!' she crowed. 'I knew he couldn't do it!'

'He *did* do it.' Jordan pointed up at the baggy shorts flying in the wind. 'He ran your shorts up the flagpole, just like he said he would.'

There was a murmur of agreement from 4K. It was quickly silenced as Big Emily shot them a beady-eyed glare.

'You two are really getting on my nerves,' Big Emily said through her teeth.

Just as she moved menacingly towards Jordan, a door was flung open.

'What *on earth* is going on here?'

Mrs Fine sailed into view, followed closely by Miss Kinsella. They both looked red with fury. Alex froze on the stairs, his legs almost giving way beneath him. 4K looked scared, and huddled closer together. Meanwhile, Big Emily's mates slunk off quickly round the corner of the school, leaving their leader to face the music on her own.

'Did I or did I not say that the back of the school was out of bounds?' Mrs Fine snapped.

'Yes, Miss,' 4K chorused miserably.

'And did I or did I not say that anyone breaking that rule would get a month's detentions?'

'Yes, Miss,' 4K agreed.

Miss Kinsella was staring at Alex standing on the fire escape. She nudged Mrs Fine.

'Jordan King!' Mrs Fine's eyes almost popped out of her head. 'So Mr Graham was right,' she muttered to Miss Kinsella. 'He did see someone on the flat roof. I thought that 5J was getting to him.' She eyeballed Alex sternly. 'Would you care to tell me what you're doing up there, Jordan?'

Alex hung his head. 'I ran Big Emily's shorts up the flagpole, Miss,' he muttered.

'What!' Mrs Fine looked up at the pink shorts flapping in the wind. Then she glared at Big Emily. 'I might have known you were involved, Emily Collins.'

'It was his idea,' Big Emily complained, pointing at Alex.

'I am sorry to say, Jordan, that you have been nothing but trouble all morning,' Mrs Fine declared sternly. 'Miss Kinsella has been telling me about your behaviour in class, and I have to say that I have never—no, never—heard of a new boy who has shown such a disregard for the school rules from the minute he walked through the gates—'

Alex was too weak and trembling to defend

himself. He just hung on to the handrail, staring helplessly at Mrs Fine.

'He's not Jordan, Miss,' Jordan said. The game was up now. They'd just have to take their punishment and grin and bear it. 'I am. He's Alex.'

Mrs Fine and Miss Kinsella glanced at each other.

'Don't be ridiculous, Alex,' Miss Kinsella said loudly.

'It's true, honest,' Jordan protested. Suddenly an idea popped into his head, and he turned to Alex. 'Alex, what's 63 x 51?'

'3,213,' Alex said immediately, and sat down on the bottom step before his legs gave way altogether.

'And this was your idea of a *joke*?' Mrs Fine's voice dripped ice. She glanced from Jordan to Alex. 'Pretending to be each other?'

'Yes, Miss,' Jordan muttered.

He and Alex had been hauled off to Mrs Fine's study to explain themselves, along with

Miss Kinsella. Jordan guessed gloomily that he wasn't going to get on very well at Maple Bank Junior, now all this had come out. So much for making a fresh start.

Mrs Fine slapped her hand down on the blue and red folders lying on her desk.

'I can understand our mistake, of course,' she snapped. 'Thanks to Mrs Binns mixing up the photographs.' Jordan thought that Mrs Binns was probably in for a telling-off later, too. 'But *really*. To go on pretending to be each other!' Her eyes bored into Jordan. 'I suppose all this was *your* idea?'

Jordan opened his mouth to say something, but he didn't get the chance.

'No, it was my idea too,' Alex said.

Mrs Fine and Miss Kinsella stared at Alex. Jordan was startled, too. Why was Alex taking the blame as well? He could easily get himself out of trouble by saying that Jordan had forced him into it.

'It was Jordan's idea at first,' Alex went on, 'but then I started joining in. Actually, Jordan wanted to stop, but I didn't want to.'

Mrs Fine looked puzzled. Alex Jackson's notes had said that he was a quiet, well-behaved boy who never got into trouble.

'Big Emily's shorts were my idea,' Alex said. 'I was just showing off in front of the other kids, so they'd like me. But then I got stuck, and Jordan had to help me down from the roof. So he's a hero, really.'

Jordan King a hero? None of his previous teachers had ever said anything like *that* before. Mrs Fine was beginning to feel all muddled. Things weren't turning out the way they were supposed to.

'I think you two had better go and have your lunch,' she said weakly. 'Starting tomorrow, you will go to the detention room every lunchtime and write lines until further notice.'

Miss Kinsella led the two boys out. Alone, Mrs Fine leaned back in her chair, and closed her eyes.

'Mrs Binns,' she called through to the school secretary, 'bring me a cup of coffee, please. And make it an extra-strong one.'

* * *

'I want to speak to you two before you go to lunch,' Miss Kinsella said.

She looked curiously at Jordan and Alex. Who would have thought meek and mild little Alex Jackson would have had the nerve to stand up to Big Emily Collins? And Jordan King, too. He was a hero, according to Alex. There was more to both of these boys than met the eye.

Miss Kinsella cleared her throat. 'I just want to say,' she began, 'that I think we should forget all about today. I think we should make a fresh start tomorrow.'

'Really, Miss?' Alex and Jordan said together.

Miss Kinsella nodded. 'Let's pretend that today never happened,' she suggested, 'and that tomorrow is really your first day. Then you can impress me with how well-behaved you are.'

'I can probably be well-behaved some of the time, Miss,' Jordan said, looking worried. 'But I don't know if I can be well-behaved *all* the time. I've never done it before.'

'Well, you can try,' Miss Kinsella said encouragingly. She was going to make sure that Jordan King worked hard and didn't spend all his time fooling around. She was also going to make sure that Alex Jackson made friends, and wasn't bullied or picked on. 'And remember, if you have a problem with *anyone* in this school—' They all knew she meant Big Emily Collins. '—then you come straight to me. Is that understood?'

Alex and Jordan nodded.

'I can't believe we got off that easily,' Jordan said cheerfully, as they went over to the canteen.

'We didn't,' Alex reminded him. 'We got a whole load of detentions, and millions of lines to write.'

'Nah, don't worry about that,' Jordan replied. 'I've invented this really cool way of tying three pens together. It makes writing lines a lot quicker.'

'Three times quicker,' Alex pointed out mathematically.

They joined the end of the dinner queue.

'I'll show you that trick with the pens when we get back to class,' Jordan said. 'And maybe you could help me with my maths sometimes.'

'Does that mean we're still going to sit next to each other?' Alex asked.

'I suppose so,' Jordan said, looking a bit surprised.

They stared at each other. Alex was thinking that he'd never had a friend like Jordan before,

and Jordan was thinking exactly the same thing about Alex. It occurred to both of them, at just the same moment, that it might be quite exciting.

OTHER OXFORD FICTION YOU MIGHT ENJOY:

One Girl School

ISBN 0 19 275173 5

Jon Blake
Illustrated by Tony Ross

Bernie is very popular. She's only just started at
Marnover School and already she's the paintbrush
monitor, the pencil monitor, and captain of the
football team. There's just one catch.

She's the only pupil!

Can Bernie cope with one headmistress, three
teachers, one caretaker, and one school cook—all
by herself? And can the school survive—with just
one pupil?

So You Want to Be the Perfect Family?

ISBN 0 19 275233 2

Josephine Feeney
Illustrated by Rachel Merriman

Are you happy with your family?
If not, would you like to change it?
Would you let television cameras into your
home to record
these changes?
We are searching
for a family to
transform into the
PERFECT
FAMILY ...

Katie doesn't think her
family are too bad. But they're not perfect. So this
TV show is the chance of a lifetime. But can the
experts *really* make them perfect? And do they
want *everybody* watching while they do it?

How to Survive Summer Camp

ISBN 0 19 275230 8

Jacqueline Wilson
Illustrated by Sue Heap

Typical! Mum and Uncle Bill have gone off on a swanky honeymoon, while Stella's been dumped at Evergreen Summer Camp. Guess what? She's not happy about it!

Things get worse. Stella loses all her hair (by accident!), has to share a dorm with snobby Karen and Louise, and is forced into terrifying swimming lessons with Uncle Pong! It looks as if she's in for a nightmare summer—how can Stella possibly survive?

NOW AVAILABLE IN A SPECIAL LIMITED EDITION WITH FREE FUNKY TATTOOS!

MEET SIMONE WIBBERLEY!

Simone's Letters

ISBN 0 19 275222 7

Simone's Diary

ISBN 0 19 275210 3

Simone's Website

ISBN 0 19 271903 3

Helena Pielichaty
Illustrated by Sue Heap

*Dear Mr Cakebread . . . For starters, my name is
Simone, not Simon . . . Mum says you sound just like
my dad. My dad, Dennis, lives in Bartock with his
girlfriend, Alexis . . . My mum says lots of ruder things
about her because Alexis was one of the reasons my
parents got divorced (I was the other) . . .*

When ten-year-old Simone starts writing letters to
Jem Cakebread, the leading man of a touring
theatre company, she begins a friendship that will
change her life . . . and the lives of all those around
her: her mum, her best friend Chloe, her new
friend Melanie—and not forgetting Jem himself!

Get to know Simone in these three wonderful,
funny books. She might just change your life, too!

The Tales of Olga da Polga

ISBN 0 19 275130 1

Michael Bond
Illustrated by Hans Helweg

From the very beginning there was not the slightest doubt that Olga da Polga was the sort of guinea pig who would go places.

Olga da Polga is no ordinary guinea pig. From the rosettes in her fur to her unusual name, there's something special about Olga . . . and she knows it!

Olga has a wild imagination, and from the minute she arrives at her new home, she begins entertaining all the other animals in the garden with her outrageous tales and stories—but she still has time to get up to all kinds of mischief and have lots of wonderful adventures, too.

More books about Olga da Polga:

Olga Meets Her Match   ISBN 0 19 275132 8
Olga Carries On   ISBN 0 19 275131 X
Olga Takes Charge   ISBN 0 19 275133 6
Olga Moves House   ISBN 0 19 275129 8